A Doll *for* Lily Belle

A Doll

for Lily Belle

Dorothea J. Snow

Illustrated by Nedda Walker

HOUGHTON MIFFLIN COMPANY BOSTON

The Riverside Press Cambridge

With Love

to

Mary Ann

A Doll for Lily Belle

A FAR PIECE up the broad new highway that winds over Dogwood Mountain there sets an old log cabin. Lily Belle Ledbetter lives there with her Mammy and Pappy and pet pig, Penelope. Only Lily Belle calls her Pennylope.

In Pennylope's ear there is a notch, close to the tip, that shows she belongs to the Ledbetters and no others.

One fine morning in early spring Lily Belle, pail in hand and Pennylope trailing, started for the well not far from the cabin. Creak! went the windlass as she turned it around and around and drew the wooden bucket on the end of the rope to the top. All the while she kept her eyes on the broad new highway that ran in front of her home.

The highway had opened up a whole new world for the Ledbetters, and for other mountain people along its way, with its cars and buses from faraway places whizzing up and down it.

"Mammy and me could set on the stoop all day and just look at the cars go by," Lily Belle said to Pennylope as she watched a bright red convertible disappear among the trees up the road. She yanked the wooden bucket up and out and splashed the clear, cold water into her pail. "But we can't do that and the washing all at the same time."

She picked up the pail of water and carried it around to the back of the cabin. She emptied it into the black washpot that stood on three legs above the fire.

Mammy was bent over the washboard, scrubbing and wringing. Lily Belle picked up a pile of wrung-out white things on the bench beside Mammy's tub and dropped them, one by one, into the washpot. An hour later she would take them out, as white as the blossoms of the dogwood trees that now looked like drifted snow on the mountainside.

"Washing is a sight of work," said Lily Belle, "without one of those electric washing machines with a wringer on top. Wouldn't one look fine on our front stoop?"

Mammy nodded. "And we could set by it and rock and watch the cars go by while it did all the work." She sighed. "But they cost a sight of money. It'll be forever, I reckon, before we get one."

With a wooden stick Lily Belle swished the clothes around in the steaming water of the pot. Mammy was right. The cheapest washing machine in the mail-order catalogue was eight'-nine dollars and ninety-five cents! And, though Mammy had been saving for quite a spell, there was only fourteen dollars and fifty cents in the old cracked pitcher on the mantel above the fireplace. Mammy put there all that was left each week of the egg money and Pappy put there all he could spare.

"If only we could get the money for one of them, quicker than forever, that is," said Lily

Belle as she chased Pennylope away from the washpot.

"I know how we can do it," said Pappy from behind her. He had just come in from plowing the cornfield to get a drink of water. "Sell that good-for-nothing Pennylope!" His voice was grim as he added, "Folks raise hawgs for meat or to sell, not for pets."

He turned and left.

Lily Belle squeezed her eyes real tight trying to shut out the picture Pappy had painted. It was a true one, she knew. A few months of fattening in the pen and Pennylope would bring a right nice price, likely, enough for the washing machine, or thereabouts.

Pennylope made into side meat and fatback! Oh, no! Mammy wouldn't want that either. She knew how much Pennylope meant to Lily Belle.

"That's enough water and fire for now, Lily Belle," Mammy said softly. "I'll holler when I need more."

Lily Belle knew what Mammy wanted her to

do. She went back around the cabin and sat down on the front stoop. Chin in hand she looked at the highway and thought real hard.

"If I had a stand up there by the road," she said to Pennylope, "and something to sell on it, likely I could make enough money to help Mammy get that washing machine."

What could she make-do that would sell? She couldn't crochet rugs, or make baskets, or whittle whistles in the shapes of birds, or polish quartz and make it into rings and brooches and such.

All these bits of mountain make-do were displayed on stands in front of cabins hereabouts. But they were all on back dirt roads where not many cars went by. Here she was, living on this beautiful highway, where cars went by thicker'n ants at a picnic, and she had neither stand nor anything to sell on one!

Her gaze turned from the road and drifted down to a little cabin in a hollow. Granny Honeycutt lived there all by herself. Granny was outside now, her sunbonnet flopping up and down, working in her garden patch. She was digging into the earth with a forked stick and dropping seeds as she went. Lily Belle knew the ground wasn't worked proper for seeds. But Granny was too old and crippled to do that kind of work.

"I'd go down and help her if I could," Lily Belle said to Pennylope, "'cause I like to neighbor with people. But Pappy says no Ledbetter has had no truck with no Honeycutt for nigh onto fifty years, and it ain't starting now."

Once Lily Belle had asked, "What did the ruction start over, Pappy?"

"I don't rightly know," he had answered sharply. "But one thing is sartin sure, it was the Honeycutts that was a-faulting."

Lily Belle sighed. Pappy was so sot in his ways.

Then she did as always at such worrisome times. She went into the cabin and picked up the wishing book. It was a big mail-order catalogue and was all the mail the Ledbetters ever got and it came twice a year.

She took the book out onto the stoop and sat down beside Pennylope. She opened the catalogue to a page she had looked at so often the edges were raggedy.

On it was the picture of a big, walking, talking, curly-haired doll, all tyked out in a pink organdy dress with a skirt that stood out like butterfly wings.

"Ain't that a fair sight?" she asked, holding the page so Pennylope could see. Never in all her born days had she seen such a doll, or expected to get one. "It does pleasure me a heap to look at it."

She kept looking at it, and the cars, until Mammy called her to put more wood on the fire under the washpot.

Evening came. Mammy and Pappy and Lily Belle sat on the stoop for a spell. The smell of freshly plowed earth filled the soft night air. Pappy looked up the mountain. He watched a big, fat, butter-colored moon climb up over the

tops of the trees. He said solemnly, "It's the light of the moon. I'm aiming to plant my corn patch come morning."

Mammy nodded. "I'm seeding my bean patch tomorrow, too," she said.

Lily Belle knew why. Seemed a body was born knowing that plants with the eating part growing above ground, like corn and beans and such, were best off planted in the full of the moon. And plants with the eating part growing underground, like 'taters and goobers and turnips, did better when planted in the moon dark.

She chimed in, "And I'm going to plant my gourd seeds all along the old rail fence!"

Pappy snorted. "Why in tunket do you want to seed more of them good-for-nothing gourds? There's enough hanging in the loft right now to last us for dippers and such for the next ten years."

Lily Belle knew she needed a reason, a good one, to plant more gourds. Then and there one popped into her mind.

"I'm fixing to set up a stand by the road," she said, "and sell my gourds there."

Pappy leaned back and laughed so hard the echo was late coming back down the mountain. He shook as he asked, "Now who do you figger is going to BUY gourds?"

Lily Belle turned blue eyes on him, full force.

"Recollect that woman that stopped for water

last summer and saw my gourds and bought eight of them and paid me two dimes, cash money?" she asked. "She said she was going to paint them and hang them in her cook-room for pretties."

"Flighty females!" Pappy clucked disgustedly.

"And that man hunter who paid me a dime for two big gourds and allowed they would make fine bird houses?"

"Musta been kicked by a mule!"

"The vines look pretty on the fence, Pappy, and the gourds, too, when they are ripe, a-hanging there all goldy-like."

Pappy snorted again. "Just like your Mammy seeding them morning-glory vines around the stoop. Planting weeds, that's what it is."

"But gourds and morning-glories ain't weeds."

Pappy thrust a long finger under Lily Belle's nose.

"Ary a thing I plant and can't eat or sell or feed to the critters is weeds," he said.

"Pennylope eats gourds when they're soft,

11

Pappy," Lily Belle reminded him.

Pappy clucked disgustedly, rose and started to go into the cabin. "That good-for-nothing Pennylope," he muttered. "What's the tarnation use of keeping her if you ain't going to eat her or sell her?" He shook his head. "If'n women ain't the beatingest critters!"

He stopped in the doorway and turned and said sternly, "Tomorrow I want to see that Pennylope in the pen with the other critters. I ain't fretting to see her rooting and tromping in my corn patch."

"I'll put her in the pen, Pappy," Lily Belle promised. Her heart sank as she said it. Pennylope wasn't going to like being penned up after roaming about at will all winter. But then, neither had the other pigs. She'd miss Pennylope, too, trailing after her everywhere she went.

Next morning she lifted Pennylope into the pen with the other critters. Pennylope squealed angrily. She ran around inside the pole pen hunting for a soft spot in the earth through which she could root her way out.

From behind the cabin Lily Belle dragged two of Pappy's sawhorses. She put them in the shade of two big oak trees out by the road. Across the sawhorses she laid a wide plank.

On another board, with pokeberry juice and a hickory twig brush, chewed real soft, she painted, "GOURDS FOR SALE." She hung this from a branch of one of the trees so it could be seen plain from the road.

She went to the loft of the cabin. From the rafters she took ten of the nicest yellow gourds. Carefully she laid them out on the plank across the sawhorses. Then she sat down on an old splint-bottomed chair she had dragged from the stoop. She sat and waited for folks to stop and buy.

Fifteen cars whizzed up the road, or down. But not one of them stopped at the stand with gourds for sale.

Lily Belle was a little put out. "I'll plant my

gourd seeds just the same," she told herself. "I can see the stand from the old rail fence and I can come if a car stops."

When the noon meal was over Lily Belle washed the dishes and went down by the fence. In the pocket of her apron were seeds she had saved from last year's gourds. She made little hills in the rich black earth and planted three gourd seeds in each one.

After seeding each hill she looked down at it with a scowl. Then she said, as angrily as she could, "You low-down, mean, ornery old gourd seeds, don't you ever come up 'cause if you do I'll beat the tar out of you!"

She had to do that. Everybody knew that gourd seeds had to be given a good cussing or they wouldn't grow worth anything.

Several cars growled up the highway but none of them stopped at the stand.

"Folks don't seem to be hankering to buy gourds today," Lily Belle said to no one in particular. Seemed queer not to have Pennylope grunting along behind her agreeing with everything she said.

She looked down at the little cabin in the hollow. Granny Honeycutt was out in her garden patch again, scratching and seeding. Suddenly Lily Belle did something she had never dreamed of doing before. She waved at Granny Honeycutt! And Granny Honeycutt waved back!

"Howdy, Lily Belle," came a voice from behind her. She jumped a foot. Was that Pappy? Had he seen her having truck with a Honeycutt?

She turned and saw Dama Lou Barkus. Dama Lou was carrying one of the beautiful rugs she crocheted from burlap bags, raveled and dyed.

"I hear tell you have a stand by the highway?" she asked.

"You heard right," said Lily Belle. "But I haven't sold any gourds yet."

Dama Lou held out the rug. "If you can sell this for three dollars I'll give you twenty-five cents of it," she said, explaining, "there just ain't any cars come by on that back road I live on."

"I'll be right proud to put it on my stand," said Lily Belle. A quarter, cash money, was a quarter!

Lily Belle hung the rug on a rope tied between the two trees, right above her stand. That afternoon a car stopped and a lady got out and bought the rug. She paid Lily Belle three dollars for it. She didn't even look at the gourds.

Right after supper Lily Belle lit out down the back path toward Dama Lou's house. She gave Dama Lou two dollars and seventy-five cents and Dama Lou gave her two more rugs to sell, a big round one and a small oval one.

On the way back home Lily Belle looked them over carefully.

I'd sure be proud, she thought, if I could make-do something as pretty as this to sell on my stand.

But she could think of nothing she could make-do with what she had.

Next morning Lily Belle was selling the last of Dama Lou's rugs when she heard another voice from behind her.

"Good morning, Lily Belle," it said.

She turned to see Emmy Leatherwood, who lived down on the creek not far from Dama Lou. On her arm hung three baskets, woven of buckbrush roots, boiled, peeled and dyed. They were as pretty as anything left by the Easter rabbit.

"I heard you had a stand up by the highway," said Emmy shyly. "Would you put these baskets on it and try to sell them for fifty cents apiece? I'll give you a nickel on every one you can sell."

Those baskets should be easy to sell. A nickel was a nickel.

"I'd be right proud to put them on my stand, Emmy," said Lily Belle. She arranged them on the plank as Emmy left. She had just sold one when a big old mountain rain marched up the road. The baskets would have been ruined if she hadn't grabbed them and taken them to the cabin. After the rain she put them back on the stand and sold the other two before noon. But nobody bought any gourds.

The days passed. Rain fell softly. The sun shone warmly down on the black earth. Tiny shoots of corn plants popped out of the ground. So did bean plants and gourd. Pennylope found a soft spot in the earth beneath the pole pen and rooted herself a trench and scooted out. Lily Belle was hard put to catch her.

Twice more it rained hard and Lily Belle worked like a squirrel getting ready for a hard winter as she saved the rugs and baskets on her stand.

A lot of cars stopped at the stand. She sold five more rugs for Dama Lou and fifteen baskets for Emmy. And she sold ten bird whistles for Eddie Thomas, who had brought them over as soon as Dama Lou and Emmy had passed the good word. Eddie gave her a quarter for selling them and she put it into the cracked pitcher along with the two dollars and ninety cents she had made off the other things.

With what Mammy and Pappy had been able to add to the washing machine money, there was now twenty-three dollars saved.

Eva Lacey and her Mammy brought over some of the rings and brooches and bracelets they made and Lily Belle put them on the stand. It was doing a good business in everything but gourds. Lily Belle was making some money from the things she sold for the others. But not nearly as much as she would have if she had had something of her own to sell.

One lady did stop and buy four gourds and paid her a quarter for them. "I shall dig a hole in one end of each gourd," the lady said, "and scoop out the seeds and fiber. Then I'll put in several pebbles and a wooden handle in the hole and have a rhythm instrument called a maracas."

Lily Belle had smiled politely and allowed to herself that the lady could make a maracas out of a gourd if she wanted to.

The corn plants tasseled and tiny ears formed. The bean plants and the gourd vines blossomed. The gourd blossoms dropped off, leaving gourds no bigger than thimbles, hundreds of them, it seemed to Lily Belle.

They looked mighty pretty on the fence and Lily Belle reckoned now that was all they were good for.

One day Lily Belle took a stroll down the road toward Granny Honeycutt's cabin. She passed Granny's old barn, which set right on the highway and at the edge of the Ledbetter land. It was a sturdy barn though it hadn't been used for a long time.

Lily Belle kept listening for the sound of a car coming up or going down the road.

In no time at all she was standing in front of Granny's cabin. Granny was sitting on her front stoop, rocking.

"Howdy, ma'am," said Lily Belle, to her own surprise.

Granny fanned herself briskly with a big cardboard fan with a picture of a pretty girl and a sack of flour and the words "Baker's Best" across the top.

"Howdy, Lily Belle," she said. "Come in and set a spell."

"Don't mind if I do," said Lily Belle. "Land, it's hot."

She squared her shoulders and walked up the steps of Granny's stoop just like she had been doing it all her life.

She was having truck with a Honeycutt and

she knew it. But just once wouldn't hurt anybody, she told herself.

She sat down. Neither she nor Granny said anything for a moment. Then Granny asked her what she had planted along the old rail fence.

"Gourds," said Lily Belle.

Granny nodded. "I used to raise gourds my own self," she said. "But I'm too old and crippled for sech now."

There was another dry spell of talk. Lily Belle spied a mail-order catalogue lying on the floor beside Granny's rocker. Likely Granny spent a lot of time wishing on it.

She picked up the book. She showed Granny the picture of the wonderful doll that walked and talked and closed its eyes when you laid it down.

"It pleasures me mightily to look at it," Lily Belle smiled. Then she added, "I never had a doll and don't reckon I ever will, less'n," she paused and giggled, "one of my gourds turns into one."

She looked up at Granny. "Would you like

some of my gourds?" she asked.

Granny shook her head. "It wouldn't pleasure your Pappy any knowing you were here, Lily Belle," she said. "I shouldn't have allowed you to come in today, but I like to visit with young folks. Anyway I have all the gourds I need."

Lily Belle rose. "I'd best be going," she said, a lump in her throat. Granny was telling her not to come again!

Then she saw Pappy coming down the road. She lit out around the cabin. There was a clearing back of it. Best not to let Pappy see her going across that.

She flattened herself against the back of the cabin. I'll bide here till Pappy goes by, she told herself.

Lily Belle couldn't see Pappy but she knew he was stalking along, looking neither to the right nor the left. He always passed Granny Honeycutt's cabin that way, though he was friendly as a waggle-tail pup to everybody else.

She couldn't see Granny either, but she knew

the old woman was sitting there, rocking and paying no mind one way or the other. That was why a body could have knocked her over with a pussywillow when she heard Granny say, in a loud and clear, though quavering voice, "Howdy, Luke Ledbetter!"

Granny was trying to get Pappy to bury that rusty old hatchet. Granny must like me a heap to do that, Lily Belle thought, swallowing the lump. She's a prideful body, too.

She strained her ears to hear Pappy's reply.

Crunch. Crunch. The sound of Pappy's footsteps on the berm of the road was all she heard. She fled.

Next day she wandered down by the old rail fence, feeling sad indeed. Gourds were hanging on the vines as thick as grapes. But the sight of them didn't pleasure Lily Belle at all.

I'll have to throw most of them away, come frost, she grieved. Pappy was right. Gourds are good for nothing but dippers.

She sat down on a stump, longing for Pennylope rooting and snorting around her. But Pennylope was in the pen with the other hawgs, as unhappy as she was. And Granny Honeycutt. Likely she'd do no more waving after the way Pappy had cut her dead yesterday.

She looked toward Granny Honeycutt's cabin. She was just in time to see Granny's tiny figure scooting down a path that led from the old rail fence. What in tunket had she been doing up here so close to the Ledbetters?

Lily Belle put her hand down beside her on the stump. It hit something and knocked it off. She leaned over and picked it up. It was a doll!

Lily Belle knew right away that it was made of a gourd. Under the face, which smiled at her from the small end of the gourd, a tiny flirty sunbonnet was tied. The full-skirted dress, made of a printed flour sack, had tiny yellow roses all over it.

"It's cuter than chigger britches!" Lily Belle giggled, hugging it to her. "Granny sure knows how to make-do."

Roasting-ear time came and went. Snap beans passed and the Ledbetters were eating leather-breeches, or shell beans dried and cooked, hulls and all. The gourds on the vines turned from green to yellow.

The coins in the cracked pitcher now amounted to thirty dollars. Lily Belle counted them one day and said sadly, "Mammy is right. It will take forever to get that washing machine."

Lily Belle sat under one of the big trees by her stand playing with her gourd doll. She was thinking on Granny Honeycutt and wondering if Granny Honeycutt was thinking on her. It was a soft, warm day in late summer, with a touch of autumn in the air. For such a day Lily Belle was feeling right low.

Summer would soon be over. Before she knew it, the school bus would be coming by, picking up her and Dama Lou and Emmy and Eddie and Eve and taking them to the brick schoolhouse in Sweet Water. That would be the end of her stand! She'd make no more money for herself, or the others, until next summer.

"It's a shame, too," she told her little gourd doll, "'cause come fall the cars will be coming up here by the bucketsful to see the trees turn yellow and red and gold."

On the plank stand stood a number of gourds. Just above them swung three gay rugs. Five baskets were grouped around seven hickory whistles that looked like birds. A tray of rings and brooches and bracelets made by Eve and her Mammy lay in the center.

Long before she could see it Lily Belle heard the chuffing of a car. She stiffened, as she always did at the sound. Would the car stop? Would it buy a gourd or so, if it did?

Around the bend in the road came a blue sedan. Nearing the stand it slowed down. It stopped. Two ladies got out and walked toward Lily Belle and the stand. One lady was tall and thin and the other was short and plump.

Lily Belle rose. She set the gourd doll down on the stand among the gourds, and waited, hopefully.

"These small gourds, Myra," said the short lady, "are just the right size for noses on Halloween pumpkins."

"You are right, Ethel," said the tall lady. "How much are they?"

"Four for a dime," Lily Belle answered happily.

Ethel and Myra bought six gourds apiece. Then Ethel bought two whistles and a basket and a brooch. And Myra bought two whistles, a small ring and a rug. Then Myra spied the gourd doll. Her hands shot out and she picked it up with a cry of surprise.

"Ethel, look!" she cried. "Isn't this the sweetest thing? So typical of the mountain folk. We must take some of these back home."

Ethel looked over the doll. "Yes, we must," she said.

Myra turned to Lily Belle. "How much are the gourd dolls?"

Lily Belle gulped. She hadn't thought of selling her doll. "A dollar," she stammered. Nobody would pay a dollar for a gourd doll when gourds sold four for a dime.

"I'll take it," said Myra. She pulled a dollar bill from her straw purse and laid it on the stand.

Ethel looked among the gourds. Disappointment showed plainly on her pleasant face. "Don't you have any more?" she asked.

Lily Belle gulped again. "Not today, ma'am," she said. It didn't matter what she told them.

She would never see them again.

"When will you have more?" Ethel and Myra were insistent.

Lily Belle shrugged. "Next week, I reckon." Next week was a long way off. The ladies would be gone from the mountain by then.

"Fine!" beamed Ethel. "We'll be at the Sweet Water Motel for another ten days. We'll be back a week from today. We will want several for each of us."

They got into their blue sedan and drove away.

Lily Belle looked at the dollar in her hand. She could give Granny half of it and keep half and both would be well paid. She would get fifty cents for one gourd that way. Goldy gourds! Goldy they were indeed! She could see the coins in the pitcher mounting fast now!

Then she stopped in her tracks. How could she ask Granny to make the dolls if Pappy wouldn't let her have truck with a Honeycutt?

"Drat that old ruction that started fifty years ago!" she cried to Mammy a few minutes later.

All afternoon, when she wasn't busy tending the stand or keeping a fire under Mammy's washpot, she tried to make a gourd doll. But it was a sorry-looking thing beside the one Granny had made, and she knew it.

She took it out to show to Mammy, smeared face and sagging bonnet and all. They were looking at it when they heard a roar from the direction of the hawg pen,

"It's Pappy!" cried Lily Belle.

"Madder'n an old bear with a sore head," added Mammy.

They ran toward the hawg pen. There they saw Pappy looking angrily down at the cabin in the hollow.

"If'n that don't beat all!" he howled, throwing his old black felt hat to the ground. "That trifling Pennylope getting out of the pen and heading straight for the Honeycutt place!"

Horrified, Lily Belle and Mammy looked down toward the hollow. There went Pennylope, straight toward Granny's cabin!

"If she tromps in that old woman's garden patch," Pappy said grimly, "by gonies, anything can happen."

Taking off like a scalded cat Lily Belle went after Pennylope. She ran until she reached the fence that went around the clearing back of Granny's cabin. But she was too late. Pennylope was in Granny's garden patch rooting all over the place.

Granny came out of the cabin, broom in hand.

She's going to chase Pennylope back this way, Lily Belle thought happily. Now Pappy will see what a nice old woman she really is.

Granny chased Pennylope out of her garden patch, but not back toward the Ledbetter cabin. Oh, no! She chased her into her own hawg pen and shut the latch with a thump!

Lily Belle blinked back her sudden tears. She turned and sorrowfully walked back toward home. This was most too hard to bear. She had not only lost Pennylope but she had lost also any chance she might have had of Granny's making gourd dolls for her. If Pappy had anything to say about it the feud would now last another fifty years!

Pappy sat down at the supper table, his face as dark as a thundercloud coming over the mountain. "That old woman run that hawg into her own pen just so's she can cut another notch in its ear and say it's her'n," he growled angrily. "Then likely she'll have it butchered, or sell it."

Again Lily Belle fought back the tears. Granny have Pennylope butchered! Or sell her! Oh, no, no!

In silence Mammy and Pappy and Lily Belle began eating their meal. They had almost finished when from the front of the cabin, came a loud and clear, though quavering, voice, "Howdy, Luke Ledbetter!"

Pappy's chin almost dropped into his plate. Mammy's hand, holding the butter dish, stopped in mid-air. Lily Belle almost fell off her chair.

Granny Honeycutt! If it had been Gabriel blowing his trumpet in front of their cabin, they couldn't have been more surprised.

They rose slowly. They walked to the front door and out onto the stoop. There, at the bottom of the steps, stood the tiny, bent figure of Granny Honeycutt. In her hand was a rope, the other end of which was looped about Penny-lope's fat neck!

"Here's your hawg, Luke Ledbetter," Granny said crisply.

Pappy looked like a little boy caught in a jam jar. He was sot in his ways but he weren't a hard man.

"I'm much obliged to you, Granny Honeycutt," he said politely. "We'll give you some turnips or beans to make up for what she ruint."

"I didn't come to get paid back for anything," Granny said, sending Lily Belle a meaningful smile. Lily Belle knew then why Granny had run Pennylope into her own hawg pen. It had given her an excuse to come up here and talk to Pappy. Lily Belle's heart swelled with happiness fit to bust.

"Luke Ledbetter," said Granny, looking Pappy right in the eye, "I'm willing to forget that old ruction if you be."

Pappy snapped his long, bony fingers.

"It's a sight easier for you to forget," he said slowly, "when it was the Honeycutts that was a-faulting."

Granny drew herself up as tall as her tiny bent frame allowed. "Were you there when the ruction started, Luke Ledbetter?" she demanded.

Pappy shifted from one foot to the other, as uneasy as a cat on the ridgepole of a cabin. "It were before my time," he said.

Granny stood, arms akimbo. "Well, it weren't before my time," she snapped. She peered up into Pappy's face. "It started, you know, when one of our hawgs got out of the pen and come up here and rooted in your grandpappy's bean patch!"

Pappy shot Mammy and Lily Belle a triumphant glance.

"It did?" he said delightedly.

Granny pushed her floppy sunbonnet farther back on her snowy hair. "It sure did," she said. "And do you know what your grandpappy did with that hawg, even though it had two notches cut plain in one ear?"

Pappy dug his hands deep into the pockets of his overalls.

"It were before my time," he said warily.

Granny shook a gnarled finger under Pappy's nose.

"Yore grandpappy drove that hawg into his own pen and butchered it and et it!"

Pappy's sails flapped.

"Won't you come in and set a spell," he asked limply.

"Don't mind if I do," said Granny and she marched up the steps of the Ledbetter cabin.

"Have a bite of vittles?" asked Mammy happily.

"Don't mind if I do," answered Granny. In no time at all she was eating butterbeans and johnnycake and drinking buttermilk with a right good appetite. The Ledbetters and Honeycutts were having truck with each other at last!

Lily Belle told Granny about Ethel and Myra and how Myra had bought the gourd doll and paid a dollar for it.

Pappy leaned across the table. "You mean that little old gourd doll that Granny left on a stump by the rail fence?" he asked.

Lily Belle gulped and nodded.

"How did you know, Pappy?" she asked.

Pappy leaned back and guffawed. "My Mammy

never raised no foolish young 'uns," he said. Then, shaking his tousled head in wonderment, "A dollar for a dressed-up gourd. If'n women ain't the beatingest critters!"

Lily Belle told Granny that Ethel and Myra were coming back in exactly a week for more dolls.

"I can sell a heap of them, Granny, if you will make them," she said. Then she added hastily, "And I can make some, too, if you'll learn me how."

"Be right proud to," Granny answered. "Where are your spare gourds?"

Lily Belle took Granny up the ladder to the loft of the cabin. There she showed the old woman the gourds hanging from the rafters. Granny picked out a dozen nice ones.

"I'll help you tote 'em home, Granny," said Lily Belle.

Next week, Wednesday, Lily Belle sat happily behind her stand. Strung on a wire above the stand, just below Dama Lou's rugs, were six gourd dolls. Beneath them, on the plank with Emmy's baskets and Eddie's whistles and Eve and her Mammy's brooches and pins, were six more. They were all tyked out in sunbonnets and full-skirted dresses of pink and blue and green, some stripedy, some pokey-dotted and some plain. Lily Belle was busily making a gourd doll. Granny had taught her how to paint the face on the little end of the gourd and make the sunbonnet and dress from a printed flour sack.

Pennylope was rooting under the big tree. All the hawgs were out of the pen now, scratching for themselves in the woods, the garden stuff having all been gathered in. Pappy still called Pennylope a good-for-nothing hawg but he didn't sound so all-fired mad about it now.

"She did help us get a fine neighbor-woman," he said.

Lily Belle had never felt so happy. With the six dollars she hoped to get from the dolls on the stand there would be thirty-nine dollars in the pitcher on the mantel.

If only she could keep the stand open through the fall months! Why, Mammy would have that

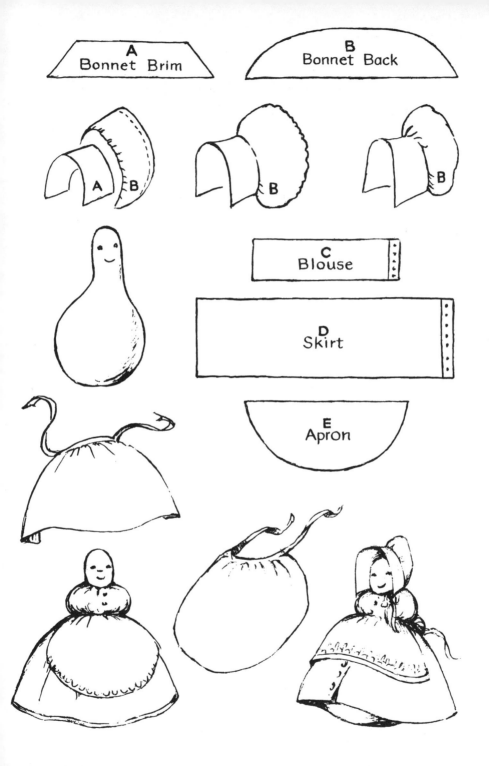

A
Bonnet Brim

B
Bonnet Back

C
Blouse

D
Skirt

E
Apron

washing machine before Christmas! But in another week the stand would have to be closed for school. It would be next summer before the beautiful machine would set on the front stoop. That would be some better than waiting forever!

"But now that I have something of my own to sell on the stand," she told Pennylope, "it just doesn't seem right to have to close down."

She listened and watched for the blue sedan.

"I reckon a body can't have everything," she sighed.

Lily Belle was so lost in thought that she did not see the big black thundercloud creeping over the mountain, nor hear the wind rising in the trees about her. The first she knew of the coming storm was when rain started falling about her in plopping drops.

"The dolls! The rugs! The baskets!" she cried in dismay, leaping to her feet. "They'll all be ruint!"

Jumping like a jaybird she gathered into her arms as many rugs and baskets and dolls and whistles and pins and rings as she could hold. Then she turned to head for the cabin.

Behind her stood Granny.

"Run for the barn!" Granny cried. "It's closer'n the cabin. Make haste! It's coming on to rain something fierce!"

The wind rose higher and the rain came down faster. In frantic haste Lily Belle headed for Granny's barn. If the rain spoiled the lovely things in her arms likely there would be no washing machine on the stoop next summer either. For she would have to take many of the coins from the pitcher to pay for the rugs and baskets and things she carried. Taking money for selling the pretties had made her responsible for them.

"Between the rain and school, running a stand just isn't worth the trouble for me," she sobbed as she went.

The barn, luckily, was a very short distance away. She reached the door, kicked it open and stumbled inside. She laid the things in her arms on the floor and ran out again. She met Granny, arms full, coming toward her, the wind wildly whipping her long skirts about her.

"Jest one more load, Lily Belle," she panted.

Just as the heavens opened and the rain came down in sheets Lily Belle laid the last of her merchandise on the floor of the barn. It rained for an hour. She and Granny stayed snug in the barn, smiling at each other.

"This barn's right handy, Granny," Lily Belle grinned. Then she added, jokingly, "Reckon I'll set up my stand in here."

They looked at each other in surprise.

"Why not?" cried Granny. "Why not a stand with a roof over it? No weather can fret you then. You're plumb welcome to my barn."

They hugged each other in pure delight.

The rain stopped. The sun came out and smiled innocently down. A car came by. Lily Belle ran to the door of the barn. She saw the blue sedan stop before the plank over the sawhorses under the trees.

"The stand's down here!" she cried and ran

toward Ethel and Myra. She led them to the barn. She showed them the dolls while Granny watched, smiling.

"We'll take all of them," said Ethel and Myra.

After they left Lily Belle and Granny divided the twelve dollars.

"That's more cash money than I have seen at one time in years," said Granny, slipping it into her pocket. "Dressing those gourds sure beats gathering ginseng in the woods."

A warm happy feeling rose in Lily Belle. Then she shook her head sadly, "Seems a shame," she said, "now that things are going so good I have to shut down my stand 'cause school is starting. Dama Lou and Emmy and Eddie and Eve and her Mammy will be mighty sorry about it too."

Granny looked thoughtful. "I'd be mighty proud to tend your stand, Lily Belle," she said softly, "while you and the other young 'uns are in school."

Lily Belle's face lit up like a Christmas tree.

"That's it, Granny!" she squealed. "That's it!"

"Let's get busy," said Granny briskly, her sweet old face glowing like a polished apple. "This here barn could stand a mite of cleaning."

Granny and Lily Belle set to work. They cleaned out the old log barn, they cleaned it out thoroughly. When Eddie brought some more whistles to sell he looked pleased and said he'd be proud to make some wooden counters and two chairs for tired folks to sit on. Dama Lou came with more rugs and when she saw what was going on she smiled happily and said she would make a nice big one for the puncheon floor. Eve said she and her Mammy would make curtains for the two windows.

"I'll make a sign for the outside," Pappy said as he looked the place over after supper. "It can hang out over the door and I'll spell out the words with sticks. Sort of rustic-like, you know."

"What'll we call it?" asked Granny.

"Mountain Make-do Barn," said Lily Belle.

"City folks won't know what that means."

"We'll call it THE MOUNTAIN CRAFT CABIN."

A few days later that was exactly what Granny's old barn had become. Lots of cars stopped and folks looked around delightedly and bought.

Granny Landis brought some of her quilts to sell. Mrs. Howard brought some of her crippled son's pottery. Soon the cabin was bulging with mountain make-do that city folks wanted to take home with them. And the cash money was more than welcome in the cabin homes on Dogwood Mountain.

THE MOUNTAIN CRAFT CABIN stays open in the fall, too, for Granny takes care of it while Lily Belle is in school. Granny does the selling and dresses gourd dolls when there are no customers.

Now on the front stoop of the Ledbetter cabin there sits a gleaming white washing machine with a wringer on top. Mammy sits in the rocker beside it, rocking and watching the cars go by. But not all the time. She crochets, too, all sorts of things like pot holders and place mats and Granny sells them at a nice profit.

Mammy says she is going to get the baby doll in the wishing book as a Christmas present for Lily Belle. Lily Belle looks pleased but says Mammy should spend her money for something a sight more needful!

Still, the pile of coins in the cracked pitcher on the mantel is beginning to grow again. And next spring more gourds will be planted along the old rail fence, as Lily Belle Ledbetter continues to make-do on the mountain.